Family Secrets
#2
Tiff's Fantasy

Chapter One

How did I go from the nerdy, picked on, shy girl to the beautiful woman every guy wanted? The woman who landed her hot step-brother? I don't know what to tell you. It confuses me too. I'll tell it the best way I can. Maybe you can make more sense of things than I can. The story began earlier in my senior year, and that's where I'll start.

Just shoot me now. Life can't get any worse. Actually, no. I better not say that. Every time I think it can't get any worse, it does. It's like saying or thinking that phrase issues a challenge to the universe, and the universe always accepts.

Let's see. Where to begin? My parents divorced five years ago. That was heartbreaking for me in more than one way. I didn't want us to be a family divided. I didn't want to have separate celebrations for all the holidays and have to walk on egg shells around my extended family. I didn't want to listen to mom's family talk about my dad and how he was the reason why the marriage ended. I didn't want to listen to dad's side put down my mom for having gained a little weight. It was a nightmare.

Then it got worse. I was old enough to choose where to live. Instead of my parents just working something out on their own, they left it up to me. Well, I chose to live with my dad. Honestly, I'd rather live with my mom, but I talked it over with her. Dad made better money and would afford a single income household better than my mom could even with any child support she may get. Most importantly, he had moved to a different school district, and that was what appealed to me the most.

This school and this town were horrible. I was picked on every single day. It was so bad in grade school, but it still managed to pick up in junior high. By the time I started high school during the middle of their divorce, I couldn't stand leaving the house. Everywhere I went I'd run into some jerk from school who made me feel like crap. I wanted to live with my dad, so I could start over somewhere new. I didn't expect popularity, but having a few friends without the constant torture from the other kids would be heaven sent.

Mom wasn't thrilled about it, but she understood. I'd visit her as often as I could. It was decided that I'd finish out the semester then I would move to dad's apartment over Christmas break. When the end of December rolled around, they let me know I would be staying put. Dad was transferring to a different position within his company and was moving three states away. They didn't want to move me so far away from everything I knew.

Move me! For the love of all that is holy, move me! That was the whole point of living with dad to begin with. I wanted to get away from everything I knew because everything I'd ever known was shit. My parents and my one and only friend were excluded from that statement of course.

I had told everyone that I was moving too. I left school at the start of Christmas break talking about how this would be the last time I had to tolerate any of their shit because I wouldn't be back. It was the worst humiliation coming back to school in January. I had anxiety about it from the time my parents filled me in on the updated plans for me. The shit I dealt with at school was twice as bad after that.

Why even give me the option of who to live with if they were going to do whatever they wanted with me anyway? It was meant to be illusion. They were certain I'd choose mom then it would look like I got to choose when I picked the home they wanted me to stay in anyway. Only I didn't do what they expected. That put a kink in their plans.

The disasters kept coming. Mom started dating again which I'm not upset about. She deserved to find a man who would treat her right. But did that man have to be Connor Newton's father?

Connor was the most handsome boy at school. He was popular, smart, an athlete, and all around perfect. Every girl had a crush on him and probably half the boys too. It was impossible not to like him. Even when he was being a douche, all he had to do was crack a smile, and whatever ill thoughts you had toward him would melt away.

Now, he was at all our family functions. It was a nightmare. Mom brought her new boyfriend and his son along with us to holidays, birthdays, weekend trips, and just random nights at home. I couldn't go to my grandparents' house without listening to them gush about what a great guy he was. Like I didn't hear enough people sing his praises at school every single day.

I can't begin to describe how much it sucked. Here was a guy on the complete opposite end of the social spectrum from me. He was everything I wasn't: good looking, smart, athletic, outgoing, and most importantly, popular. He was one of the nicer popular kids. I'll give him that. He never ran me down to my face like the other assholes, and he hadn't behind my back that I'd ever heard about. Still, he was good friends with a lot of the jerks who did.

The icing on the cake was how hot he was. When I said every

girl at school had a crush on him, I meant it. That included me. I'd never had a boyfriend. Not a real one anyway, but there had been a couple guys who had lead me on and duped me. No one at school was interested in me, and I didn't have a car until recently or a lot of friends to go elsewhere to hang out hoping to find a guy in a different district. Connor was my eye candy and had been for years. Almost every fantasy I masturbated to was about him. Well, him or that cute actor on that vampire series.

I put up with this throughout almost all of high school. It was senior year and almost to the end of the first semester. There wasn't much time left before I would be off to college and not have to deal with these idiots anymore.

My eighteenth birthday was celebrated a week late, so we could combine my party with Connor's. What a fucking terrific idea. That's when our parents dropped the real bomb on us. They were moving in together over Thanksgiving weekend which meant Connor and I would be living together too.

I don't know why they couldn't wait until after the end of the school year. It would be so much easier on everyone, especially me. Our house was technically a three bedroom, but the third room was tiny and had no closet. I was going to have to make room in my closet for some of Connor's things. It wouldn't be for his day to day clothes, but other items. They'd put an armoire in his room for that. It also meant I'd have to share the bathroom with him. Mom had her own, but the other two bedrooms shared a bath. We both had a door to it off our bedrooms. This wasn't going to be fun.

Rumors started circulating around school immediately. I guess they aren't rumors if they're true. A lot of people were asking me about it, and some had the audacity to tell me how lucky I was. One bitch even went so far as to tell me not to get my hopes up because Connor wouldn't look my way if I was the last girl on earth.

Then they moved in. It was awkward. The potential bathroom problem was addressed at a family meeting. To make sure we never walked in on each other, we were to keep the bathroom doors to our rooms locked at all times and use the hall door when we needed to get in the bathroom. That was bullshit. When I'm in my room for the night, I'm typically in a tank top and panties. I'm not putting pants on to leave my room every time I have to pee. I figured I'd just check to see if the light is on before I go in.

Family meeting? No. Our parents could get married, but Connor would never be my step-brother. He'd always be the son of my mom's husband. That's it.

On New Year's Day, they took us to a party which was the second bomb they dropped on us. It turned out the party was their wedding. It was low-key and casual with only family and a couple of their friends present. We had no warning. That's probably why they did it like that. Connor and I walked around the church banquet hall in utter shock and put on fake smiles for the guests. I couldn't eat a bite at the reception. My stomach was so tied in knots I probably would've thrown it up in front of God and everyone.

I'm sure you've probably guessed by now the reason they were suddenly moving things along so quickly after years of dating. It was bomb number three. My mom was pregnant.

I didn't know what to think anymore. I had been an only child for eighteen years. Now I was going to have a half sibling and a Connor. I overheard him on the phone talking to someone. It was one of his friends I guess. He was saying that with a baby connecting their families it was now official. We were step-siblings and would be for the rest of our lives regardless of what happened with our parents. He sounded disgusted. Glad to know I wasn't the only one entirely unhappy about the situation.

When we went back to school after the break, the shit really hit the fan. No one in a fifty mile radius hadn't heard the news. Kids who had never spoke a kind word to me in their life were now trying to buddy up to me. It was worse than the bullying. They tried to invite me to get together's at their homes. "Oh, and why don't you bring Connor?"

It made me physically ill. Or, they were trying to invite themselves over to my house. I'm not stupid. I know none of them had a drastic change of heart during the two week break from school. They were all pretending to be my friend because they wanted to get closer to Connor. Somehow they thought being at my house, being in close proximity to him, would miraculously open his eyes to how this girl was truly his soul mate. Ugh.

I spent weeks telling everyone no. Some showed up at the house unexpectedly, telling whoever answered the door I had invited them. It made for some tense confrontations when I had to tell them they needed to leave. I wasn't completely rude to them although I had every right to be after what they put me through all these years. I would say now isn't a good time because of whatever lie came to me first.

It didn't take long for the girls at school to become twice as bad in their treatment of me. They accused me of trying to keep Connor to myself, and they told me Connor would never be interested in an ugly loser like me. The rumors started flying that I had a crush on my step-brother. Nasty things were said about me, written on the bathroom walls, and passed around in notes. When that wasn't enough to break me, they started telling everyone who would listen that I had fucked him. They said I was a dirty whore who snuck into his room one night when he was drunk and took advantage of him.

Through it all, his reputation was never damaged. It actually made him cooler in a way for people to think he fucked his step-sister. It's a sexual conquest that not too many are capable of accomplishing. The same rumor made me a leper. The few people who were nice to me and chatted with me at school wouldn't even look in my direction anymore. Double standards are the ultimate bullshit.

Chapter Two

Apparently, Connor had no intention of following the rule of only using the hallway door for the bathroom either. It was a nightmare how I figured it out the hard way.

Connor is insanely hot and fit. It should be illegal to be that attractive especially when you add in his other good qualities. As much as I hate all the changes the last few years have brought, the rare chance of catching him without a shirt is probably the only perk I have. But let me be perfectly clear. I am not a pervert who is hanging around hoping to catch him with as little on as possible. I also in no way try to set up circumstances to bring us together. I know that's what everyone would think if they found out about this.

I'm pretty much what you might consider a nerd. It's not because I love school and learning so much. It's just easier to stick your nose in a book then tell your parents you have almost no friends. On the bright side, my grades are amazing, and my college prospects would make any parent beam. I spend most of my free time with my school work because I have nothing else to do.

When I'm holed up in my room, I usually listen to classical music. It's just white noise. Any other kind of music distracts me, and no music makes it too quiet and eerie. Earlier tonight, I was studying for an English test and decided to take a break. When I took the earbuds out of my ears, I thought I heard something.

It took a minute to figure out where the noise was coming from. It was Connor. He was in the bathroom, and he was singing. I couldn't hear enough to tell what song, or songs, he was crooning, but that's what he was doing. I thought it was hilarious. The water turned on and I realized he was getting in the shower. His singing got even louder, and I couldn't help but bust up laughing. I thought singing in the shower was a Hollywood concept. I didn't know people actually did it.

Then I realized he was in the shower!

The thought hit me like a ton of bricks. Connor was in the next room not more than ten feet from where I stood. He was naked and soaked with water from head to toe. The thought, and yeah, the mental image of it, made me instantly wet. I froze like a deer caught in headlights. I felt naughty like I had done something wrong, but I hadn't. Right? My heart raced, and even though I knew it was wrong, I couldn't stop getting more and more turned on over it. Knowing that it was wrong to think these thoughts about my step-brother actually made me hotter.

I gave in to them. Not my proudest moment, but it happened. I figured thoughts are harmless. People think things all the time they don't necessarily mean. It's just the rashness of the situation. If no one ever finds out my thoughts about Connor then they're not hurting anyone. Plus he'd been the source of most of my self-pleasuring fantasies since my hormones first ran rampant during puberty. That's supposed to change now that our parents had gotten hitched?

In my nightstand drawer was a small stimulator. I had it longer than I'd been old enough to buy it. That's the beautiful thing about shopping online. You can be any age, and the adult stores disguise the packages, so your mom is none the wiser.

I laid back on my bed with it and slipped it inside my panties. I glided it over my clit, rubbing it for a minute before pushing the button at the bottom to turn it on. It didn't take long to get off with this little guy, and I had something better than a fantasy. Connor was in the bare, naked flesh just on the other side of the door. I stared at the door and willed him to open it for some reason, any reason. I wanted to see him standing there, skin glistening from the water, and a towel wrapped around his waist. And of course, I wanted that towel to fall.

It was so real in my mind. The towel fell, and he scrambled to pick it up. I grabbed his hand before he could and took it from him, tossing it across my room. He looked at me confused and started to speak. All he could do was stammer. The nervousness and vulnerability of being unexpectedly naked in front of me threw him, and he didn't know what to say. I put my finger to his lips to silence him then traced my fingertips down his chest following the happy trail of hair down to his cock. I wrapped my fingers around his member and sucked in my breath from the excitement of it.

That was all it took. My body tensed up, and I felt the muscles of my pussy contract as my orgasm raged. Juices poured out of me soaking my panties even more. When it was over, I turned off the stim and stared at the ceiling wondering if I'd ever know what the real thing felt like. I'd had two sexual partners. I'd had sex before, but neither of them had made me cum. Every orgasm I've experienced was my own doing. I couldn't wait to know how it felt to have a man to bring me to the brink for a change.

The water was still running in the bathroom. I sat up and threw my legs over the edge of the bed. I looked around my room hoping to find something to use to clean up. It was the first time I'd masturbated when I couldn't just run into the bathroom afterward. While I was looking, the water turned off, and I heard Connor pull the curtain back. With any luck, he wouldn't take long to head back to his room.

A few minutes passed, and the light coming from under the bathroom door off my room disappeared. I hadn't heard him open or close the door to the hallway, but he had obviously left. I waited another minute before putting my ear to the door, but didn't hear anything. I didn't want to throw more clothes on to go into the hallway to knock, and I couldn't risk anyone seeing me dressed like this. Feeling like it was safe, I opened the door slowly and peered inside.

It was empty. I peeled my panties off and tossed them into my laundry basket. There was enough light coming from my room to see by, and I wouldn't take more than a minute. The sink was located directly across from my doorway. I turned the lock on the hall door just in case he came back in the next couple minutes.

I grabbed a washcloth from the shelf and wet it down. I was almost done cleaning up the cum that had flowed out of me minutes before when I heard Connor say, "Uh, sorry."

I spun around so fast I almost fell over. There he was standing in the doorway to his room behind me. When I saw him, he was in the process of trying to duck back out of the bathroom, but he stopped in his tracks when I turned. He looked terrified, and repeated himself, "Sorry."

His eyes glanced down then back up at my face. He swallowed hard like there was a huge lump in his throat.

'Oh my god! He had come into the room to the sight of my bare

ass, and then I treated him to a perfect view of my neatly trimmed bush.'

I wanted to scream, but when I opened my mouth, no sound came out. We stood there frozen in place for what probably amounted to several seconds, but it felt like an eternity. I ran to my room, not bothering to grab a towel to cover myself. It wasn't because he had already seen everything; it was because I was too mortified to think about getting one. The tears were flowing freely before I closed the door behind me.

It was hard to be in the same room with him after that much less look at him. The next morning, I went into the kitchen early hoping to leave the house before he even woke up. No luck. He walked in, and I grabbed my toast and headed out the back door. I didn't want to be anywhere near him. As I left, I heard him say, "Looking good, Tiff."

The tears stung my eyes again, but I fought them back. I wasn't about to go back in the house to fix my makeup if I ruined it crying. My nightmare kept growing and becoming more horrifying until it was a monster so large, I wasn't sure I could survive against it. If I never saw Connor Newton again, it would be too soon.

Chapter Three

It was excruciatingly painful to be around him for weeks after that night. The mere sight of him or the sound of his voice would bring back the memory of the look on his face the night in the bathroom. My cheeks would instantly turn beet red, and I'd feel flush and hot. I wondered if he knew. Even if he didn't suspect I had been thinking about him while pleasuring myself, he had to have seen enough to know I was cleaning up after masturbating.

I wanted the end of the semester to hurry up and arrive. I could find ways to spend my summer. I'd be leaving for college out of state in August. Until then, I could spend some time visiting dad and both sets of grandparents. It didn't matter what Connor's plans were because I could make sure we barely saw each other on my own.

It seemed like since I didn't want to run into him that was all I did. Every time I went to the kitchen for a snack, he'd appear out of nowhere. I'd go out back to sit and relax, and he'd be in the shadows. He was everywhere.

Most nights I cried myself to sleep. Between the constant berating I took at school over him living with me which I had no control over and the humiliation of being around him, it was more than I could bear.

My life had become a nightmare. I knew it wouldn't be forever. It was almost over. I counted the days. There were eighty-three days of school left when I hit the limit of what I could take. Then I could hide away over the summer until it was time to leave for college. After that, it'd be a fresh start. I'd be surrounded by people who didn't know me. They wouldn't have this fictitious past to hold against me.

Eighty-three days. The rest of January, four full months, and a few days in June. There were thirteen regular weekends, one - three day weekend, two - four day weekends, spring break, the senior trip which I planned on being too sick to attend, senior skip day and spring break. I memorized the calendar. I broke the semester down into quarters, the quarters into weeks, the weeks into days, and the days into hours. Every Monday I psyched myself up for the week. I just needed to make it through this class. I only had to last until lunch, which I spent in the bathroom. Then the day was almost over, and I'd soon be on base: my home.

Misery took on new meaning for me. I never truly knew what it felt like to be alone and in despair until then. From the beginning, I allowed myself sick days. Going off the handbook rules for how much school you can miss, I allowed myself two late arrivals, three days to leave early as well as three full days absences over the eighty-three torture filled days. My mother would never know when I missed, not these ones that I allotted myself. There's a limit to the number of absences you can have without a doctor's note. I made the calls from my mom myself. If I had to call home to leave early, I spoke to my cell phone voice mail. The office didn't ask to speak to the parent at the high school level unless it was a problem student which I was not.

I was spiraling, and I knew it. As much as I was aware of how bad it was getting, how bad I was getting, it never really sank in until after it passed. I would start each day with my scheduler. I would end each day with it. And I would look to it for support multiple times in between. My life had become centered around counting the minutes until I felt safe again.

Meanwhile, Connor was relentless. I thought he meant well. He was trying to smooth things between us, so it wouldn't be so awkward when we bumped into each other. He tried his hardest to spend time with me, but I always refused. He'd resort to using my own mom against me. From time to time, he'd suggest family nights to her, and I'd be forced to attend. It was mostly dinner out or maybe a board game at home.

Either way, I'd have to put on a happy face and endure. Sometimes I wound up having fun. For a passing moment, I'd forget about everything else, and my laugh would be pure. It was rare, and it was fleeting.

What I didn't know was Connor had an ulterior motive to all of it. How could I? There was nothing that would have made me think he was genuinely trying to get to know me better. That he had always thought I was pretty, but he ran in different circles. That he felt a spark.

Why would I, plain Jane and leper, ever think I was the object of Connor's masturbation fantasies and had been for years?

Chapter Four

I'm not in any way saying I changed my mind about Connor immediately. All I'm saying is he surprised me in a good way which isn't an easy task to accomplish. At least not when it comes to him.

Things at school had gotten pretty bad. The other kids were relentless. It wasn't just about Connor anymore. Other boys were beginning to claim they'd slept with me as well. It wasn't much of a stretch for the rest of the school to believe since they already bought into the rumors about Connor. Just like with him, these jerks added another notch to their belt so to speak. I was another conquest for them which padded out and helped them to be viewed as a stud. Meanwhile I was being thought of as a bigger and bigger slut.

I didn't witness what happened. Part of me would've liked to have seen it. The vindication. The entire romance fantasy of a knight in shining armor coming to your rescue is appealing, but to be honest, I'm glad I wasn't there. I didn't have to be present to know what happened. The entire school was abuzz with the news by the end of the next period.

Connor and I had different lunch periods, but even if we didn't, I wouldn't have been in the lunchroom to see it. My only friend has a different lunch too which means I'm alone. It had never been an issue before Connor moved in. I'd sit at the end of a table by myself. Sometimes there'd be other kids at the other end. Sometimes I'd be entirely by myself.

Since the talk about him got out of hand, I would always go thru the ala carte line. No matter how good something might look that day, I would only pick the prepacked items. As soon as I paid, I'd take them off the cart and shove them in my jacket pockets.

I'd spend my entire lunch period in the bathroom. I'd read or work on homework. My lunch was devoured quickly in the hall on the way there or back to my locker afterward. I'd hit a low point in my life, but it wasn't so low I had resorted to eating in a bathroom stall.

I had lunch after him, so on the day it happened, I was aware there was a lot more whispering going on. Whispering that was accompanied by glances in my direction and fingers pointing at me. I hadn't yet heard what the latest rumor was that must be going around about me, and at that point, I really didn't care. My curiosity was aroused in English class which was my next period, but I still had to wait to get the full scoop.

My English teacher was always a few minutes late to class. The classroom was in the old part of the high school at the very end of the building. On the other side of the classroom was his office, and in that hallway, there was an outside door that was for teachers only unless there was an emergency. Everyone knew after lunch, he stepped outside to smoke.

That's why he was late. Nobody cared. It gave the class a couple extra minutes to unwind, talk, and gossip. Not me. I usually sat with my books and notebooks out, staring straight ahead. Sometimes I'd listen in on whatever teeny bopper nonsense people were discussing. Sometimes I'd intentionally tune out the sounds of their voices.

As always, I was the first one in the classroom. I'd normally leave the bathroom and head to my locker shortly before the bell rang to dismiss lunch. I didn't like for anyone to see me shoving what could only loosely pass as lunch down my throat. Once the other kids started to arrive, the questions and comments began flying.

"Damn, girl! Who knew?"

"Did you really tell him that? Good for you!"

"You could be a #MeToo poster child. I'm serious."

"I have to admit I was wrong about you. It was pretty cool what you did."

One guy even went so far as to ask if I had a date for the Valentine's Dance. I hadn't thought Max even knew I existed.

I had no idea what was going on. All I knew was that something had happened, and for the first time in my life, it was something good.

By the end of the day, I learned the details from my friend Kara who had a damn near front row seat to the show. The pretty boys were getting loud and obnoxious at lunch like usual. That's what we called the popular guys at school. They were teasing each other and carrying on. It started as hushed comments met with roaring laughter, but the volume soon turned up.

Then one of them loudly said, "But no one compares to my man, Connor. Not too many people get to add their step-sister to their long list of conquests."

Connor said, "How many times have I told you, Derrick?"

Gabby is like the unofficial leader of the slut troop. That's what we called the popular group of whoreos who were always hanging around the pretty boys. She said, "Come on, Connor. Everyone knows."

"You don't know shit," Connor spat back.

At that point, Connor stood up on a chair and addressed the entire lunch room. "I want to make it known once and for all that Tiff Anne Ashe is an amazing person. She's incredibly smart, artistic, beautiful and incredibly funny."

If that wasn't enough, he continued. "I have never slept with her, but it's not for lack of trying. She shuts down my advances every time. She told me, 'I know you think you can get anybody, Connor, but I'm not just anybody.' The one thing Tiff is not is a slut which is more than I can say for most of you."

I couldn't believe it. Not only did he come to my defense, but he concocted a lie that made me sound like I had a lot of backbone and self-respect. Neither of which I would've counted among my traits. Most importantly though, he put his own popular status on the line to do it.

Chapter Five

I went straight home from school that day and waited for Connor to come home. I knew he had wrestling after school and wouldn't be home right away. I didn't realize he had a meet. It was just me and my mom all evening. Connor and his dad grabbed a bite to eat on the way home. By the time they got here, it was late.

I sat in my room trying to concentrate on my school work, but it was a lost cause. I spent hours pacing the floor thinking of what I would say to him when he finally came home.

Once I heard the truck pull in the drive, I went to my bedroom door and cracked it. There were footsteps on the stairs then the sound of Connor's door opening and closing behind him.

I went straight down the hall and knocked on the door, but I didn't wait for him to answer. I tried the handle, and it was unlocked.

I walked inside, and he was standing by his bed, unpacking his bag. "I don't know what to say," I blurted out. "Why did you do that?"

He tossed the notebook he was holding onto his bed and turned to me. "So you've heard then?"

"Of course I've heard. Do you even go to my school?" I asked sarcastically. "Word gets around fast. Why did you do that?" I asked again.

Connor shrugged and folded his arms across his chest, staring at his feet. "I've been telling those guys since the beginning that nothing has ever happened between us, but they told their own version of events like they always have."

He glanced at me. "I'm not an idiot you know. I've seen how far you've dipped since I moved in. I'm sure the rumors played a part in that. I'm also sure there are more rumors than the ones I know about. I'm sick of the talk as I'm sure you are too."

"Yeah, but," I swallowed back my tears. He noticed the change in me. My own mother hasn't suspected anything is wrong, but my step-brother who barely knows me could tell. "Why did you lie?"

Connor tilted his head to the side and squinted his eyes at me. "I didn't lie. We never slept together."

"You know what I mean. You said I turned you down. That never happened."

A slow grin spread across Connor's face. "But you have. You do. All the time. I just embellished it a bit."

I stood there confused. There had to be some inside meaning I was missing.

"We used to hang out a lot when I first moved in because our parents forced us too. Still, we got to know each other. When I walk in a room now, you walk right out. Whenever I try to spend time with you, you shut me down. I have to get your mom involved to see you more than the three seconds it takes you to disappear through a doorway."

There was a silence that draped over us while I tried to find words, any words at all to say. "Who knows what might've happened between us if we had hung out," Connor winked. "I meant the things I said about you."

"I don't know what to say," I repeated. And I didn't. No one had ever stood up for me like this before. It was unchartered territory.

"Well I do," Connor said. "You're welcome."

I don't know what came over me in that moment. It was likely a combination of factors. I had been seeing Connor so much all these months. Sometimes he was shirtless. Sometimes he was in those gray sweatpants. Fantasizing about him while I took care of my own needs as I had been doing long before he moved in. Listening to the talk at school claiming we had slept together. Even though we hadn't, even though it was something that would never happened, hearing it repeated for so long and so often put the idea in my head and made it seem like it was a possibility at times.

There was something about the way he stood there with that cocky attitude. His body still smelled of sweat from his wrestling meet. Maybe it was the way his hair fell over his forehead because he was overdue for a trim. Whatever *it* was, it took over me. Without thinking, without hesitation, I kissed him. I planted my lips firmly on his and kissed him hard.

As if that wasn't enough, it wasn't the terrifying part. Connor kissed me back. Moments had passed before I realized his tongue had found its way into my mouth and was dancing with mine. When he moved to wrap his strong muscular arms around me, I pushed him away.

"Thank you," I breathlessly whispered and ran out of his room.

Chapter Six

For weeks after the kiss, things were normal. Sound unbelievable? Yeah, it was a little unbelievable to me too.

Connor never mentioned it. Not once. I assumed it was because he knew it was a spur of the moment thing, but more importantly, it was something that shouldn't have happened. He was doing me a favor by forgetting about it instead of making things more awkward between us by bringing it up again.

Where we were concerned, things started to fall back in place at home, only better. We started hanging out more. I stopped running away every time he appeared. We didn't even need our parents forcing us to spend time together anymore. It became more natural. We became friends.

And Max, the guy who asked if I had a date to the dance... Well, I accepted. He asked me out the following Monday, and I owe that to Connor too. Max told me he always knew I was pretty, but he never saw me as girlfriend material until Connor spouted off all those great qualities about me.

I'm not sure how I felt about what he said. I didn't know, and still don't know, if I should be upset about it. Does it matter how he came to be interested in me? Shouldn't it only matter how he treats me? This is probably one of those things I'll look back on and regret being so ignorant, but for right now, I'm enjoying having a boyfriend who isn't ashamed of me.

I won't lie. I had kind of hoped the kiss with Connor might

make him see how much he wanted me, and he'd ask me out. I knew it was a stretch. We were step-siblings now, like it or not. Was a relationship really something we should be considering even if we both wanted it?

If it didn't work out, we'd have that stain on the family forever. Stain might be a harsh word, but you get the point. What if we tried for it, and everything came up roses? Mom was pregnant. We'd have to tell that child his brother and sister were together. It was a soap opera if you think about it.

It made me take a bigger interest in myself, my appearance. I started wearing makeup all the time which meant I started wearing it to school. In the past, I didn't want to waste my good looks on such foul creatures. Things changed, and I liked the attention I was getting. It was good attention.

Max was treating me right. He took me out a couple nights a week, and I was looking forward to the dance. I was prepared for him to try to get down my pants that night. Actually, I was hoping he would. It was a little disappointing that he hadn't made a move yet.

The night of the dance I looked good. I still had the dress I wore to my cousin's wedding the year before, and it fit perfectly. No one at school had ever seen me in it, so I wore it. Her colors had been red and black, so this red dress was perfect for a Valentine's Dance. When Max picked me up, I could tell by his reaction it had the desired effect.

I spent the whole night a little too close to him while keeping an eye on the chaperones to make sure they didn't say anything about it. We wouldn't have been in any trouble. They'd just tell us to create space between us, but I didn't want to make Max nervous in a bad way. I didn't want him trying to shoo me away on his own thinking they'd catch us again. I only wanted to make him nervous in the way that might help us get even closer after the dance.

Connor was there too. He came stag which bewildered everyone, myself included. I might not have said it to him, but it was true. He could have anyone he wanted. The few whoreos who came together instead of with dates hovered over him all night. It was pathetic. You could smell the desperation on them. They all wanted to be the one he left with and hopefully got to know better while parked on the side of some country road.

I didn't get the chance to see who he picked. Max and I were out on the floor for a slow dance, and we were a little closer than was allowed. I rubbed his groin with my body every chance I got, and I had ample opportunities. Finally, he broke free of me and asked, "You're doing that on purpose, aren't you?"

I smiled and nodded, biting my lower lip.

"Are you sure about this?" he asked.

I wrapped my arms around his neck and began to sway again to the music. "Very sure," I whispered in his ear.

He moved so fast I nearly fell over. He took my hand and led me out of the gym. I could barely keep up with him in my heels, but he didn't slow down till we reached his car.

Max checked the time on the dash when he turned the key and announced, "Good. We've got two hours."

"Two hours? What?"

He grinned impishly at me. "My mom's a nurse and works second shift. It will be two hours before her shift ends, and who knows how long after that till she gets home."

I already knew it was just him and his mom since his dad left. *Well, I'll be damned,'* I thought. *'I don't even have to suffer the cramped backseat of his used Civic.'*

We drove to his house and went inside. He tried being a proper host, asking if I wanted anything to drink and showing me around. I cut him off quick by asking, "Where's your bedroom?"

Max stepped closer and kissed me. He grabbed my hand and led me upstairs. Once inside his room, we started ripping our clothes off as if by cue. Neither of us said a word, but by then, I must've finally made it clear that not only was I ready to sleep with him, but I wanted it now.

His hands were fumbling over my skin, but he had a little bit of a previous education. I really don't have room to talk. My sexual history wasn't near enough to make me skilled. I had seen movies, read books, listened to people talk, and surfed websites that I shouldn't have been looking at before my eighteenth birthday. I knew what to do; I just didn't have the practice. I think it was the same with Max. He needed more confidence in his movements which would only come with practice, and I was willing to let him perfect his craft on me.

It had been well over a year since the last time I had sex. On top of that, I had all these months with the object of my fantasies just down the hall from me. My mind, as creative as it was, had run out of new fantasies about Connor to masturbate to. After a while, the old ones didn't do it for me anymore. I needed the real thing.

Every attempt Max made at foreplay, I blocked. His hands and mouth got swatted away or redirected over and over as I slowly walked backward toward his bed wearing only my bra and panties. Once I felt the bed touch the back of my legs, I pushed him away gently.

Reaching behind me, I unfastened my bra and let it slip down my arms then I shimmied my panties down to my ankles and kicked them away. I stood in front of him completely nude and gave him a moment to drink it in before lying back on his bed.

He finished removing his pants which required him to kick his shoes off first. He started to climb on top of me, but I pressed against his shoulder and tugged at the waistband of his boxer briefs. He looked at me sheepishly, but eventually nodded. He stood up and removed them, but not before turning off the light in his bedroom first.

'Isn't it women who are supposed to be shy?'

I heard him mutter under his breath as he tripped on something in the dark. It was probably my heels. I stifled my laugh and was thankful he couldn't see my grin.

"Do you have protection?" I asked before he joined me again.

"Yeah," he answered. "Just a sec."

I could barely make out his silhouette, but I could hear a drawer open followed by the sounds of a package ripping. He found his way back to me and propped himself up on one elbow over me. "Are you sure?" he asked again.

"Yes," I said firmly and grabbed his shoulders, pulling him closer. I locked my lips on his while he positioned himself between my legs. We were still kissing when I felt the tip of his cock penetrate me.

I turned my head and let out a moan. Max felt amazing inside me. The slow and steady rhythm was exactly what I'd been yearning for, but something was off. As much as I wanted it, as much as I needed it, I wasn't really into it.

I moaned and gasped like reciting a script. I allowed the noises escaping my lips to grow louder. I moved in time underneath him. I did everything I could do to make him believe I was enjoying myself. I didn't understand why it wasn't working.

I closed my eyes, and Connor's face flashed behind my lids. The image of him took my breath away. I couldn't get into it because it was Max who was fucking me and not my step-brother.

I began to imagine it was Connor thrusting his shaft inside me instead of Max. Pretended it was Connor's whose lips were on my neck. My moans became real in an instant. I was close, and I knew it. My first real orgasm with a guy was still going to be accompanied by fantasies of the boy I could never have. In my mind, Connor whispered, "I love you," to me.

That was what I needed to push past the threshold. My body began to convulse, and I could feel the walls of my pussy squeeze and release Max's cock over and over. It wasn't until I finished riding out the wave of my passion that I realized Max was collapsed on top of me. He'd finished as well.

Chapter Seven

When I got home that night, no one was around. It wasn't that late. In fact, I got in well before curfew. It wasn't unusual for everyone to retire to their bedrooms early to watch TV, play video games, or in my case, stick their nose in a book. I was surprised that Connor beat me home, and I was doubly surprised he wasn't in the kitchen devouring all the leftovers in the refrigerator like I expected.

I went up to my room and as I opened my door, I could've sworn I heard something. I looked around, but the hallway was empty. Even in the dim light, I could see I was alone. It sounded like a door shutting, but there had been no one in the hall with me.

In my room, I wondered if it had been Connor. Was he checking to see what time I got in? It had to be wishful thinking. It was probably my mom who was looking to see who was home.

The next day, Connor interrogated me about why I got home so late. Telling him I was home early did nothing to ease his anger. Why was he angry anyway? He knew I left the dance around nine. He saw me go and was wondering where the hell I was for almost two hours after that. I told him he wasn't my dad and to back off. It was none of his fucking business where I was or what I was doing.

Eventually, he apologized and things slowly fell into place. He had sports and friends. I had Max and Kara. Still, there were nights when we'd be in the living room, hanging out together. And it gradually evolved from there.

I'm conflicted. Max is a decent guy and all. I enjoy spending time with him, and I really enjoy the feel of his naked torso under my hands when I ride him to climax.

The problem is when we're having sex, I close my eyes and imagine its Connor bringing me to orgasm. I don't mean to do it. I don't consciously think I can't wait to have sex at the end of our date, so I can fantasize about my step-brother. It's quite the opposite actually. I spend the time leading up to sex scolding myself and swearing not to do it again. But I still do.

When we're not having sex, I'm preoccupied with wanting to get home to Connor. I know his schedule and not because I'm a stalker. It's on the calendar in the kitchen, and our parents are always discussing the logistics of where he needs to be and when. On the nights when Connor is free, I'd rather stay at home. Even if Connor is out with his friends, I want to be there waiting on him. When he's got a meet scheduled, I know when to expect him, and I don't like staying out with Max any longer than that.

It's really unfair to Max. He's such a great catch. The irony of it is he and I would've never dated if it wasn't for Connor, and he's the one who is unwittingly coming between us.

Tonight is one of those nights where I sit at home, bored out of my mind and wait for Connor to return from whatever it is he's up to. I didn't blow off Max for him at least. I don't have to feel guilty about that.

He's always home earlier than he has to be. Well, almost always. I wasn't expecting him till around 8 or 9. He'd hit the kitchen for leftovers from dinner even though he would've grabbed a bite to eat while he was gone. I wish I could eat like he did without blowing up like a whale. Then he'd cram his homework in before bed.

That's what I lived for. Pathetic? I know it is. Sometimes he'd ask me for help, especially with Chemistry. Most of the time, I just hung out in the living room while he was doing his work. His room was way too small for a desk, so he used my mom's down here. I liked being able to sneak glances at him, watch him run his fingers through his hair, and chew on his pen while he was thinking.

Yeah, definitely pathetic.

It would be hours before he showed up. I had a lot of time to kill. My school work was done. I normally spent this time studying, so I would always be prepared. Not sure why I didn't expect I wouldn't be able to sit still. I wanted the time to fly, and I knew I'd be staring at the clock, failing at any attempts to study.

It was hot in my room, so I took off my sweater to cool off and removed my bra from under my tank to be comfortable. The tank top I had on underneath it wasn't appropriate to wear by itself because it was so see-through, but that didn't matter in the comfort and privacy of my bedroom. I put my earbuds in and listened to some music while putting away the laundry mom had left on my bed. Soon, I was dancing around my room, singing along to the music that only I could hear.

I almost screamed when I turned around to see Connor standing in the doorway. When he saw me, he leaned against the frame and smiled. I quickly pulled tiff earbuds from my ears and looked around for where I laid my phone to turn my playlist off.

"You know," he chuckled. "I came home thinking you might want some company to keep you from boredom, but I see you have no end to the ways you can occupy yourself."

I turned off the music on my phone then tried to regain my composure which I failed at miserably. "Oh, ha-ha," I spat at him. "I didn't know you were there."

"I could tell," he smiled.

We stood there in silence for several moments before he asked, "Happy to see me?"

My eyes narrowed at him in confusion until he gestured toward my chest. I looked down and my hard nipples were pushing through the thin fabric of my tank top. Every inch of my breasts could be seen easily. It really left nothing to the imagination. I quickly crossed my arms over my chest.

Connor's eyes raised to meet mine, and he flashed me a striking smile. "Why don't you put some clothes on and join me downstairs, Tiff?"

With that, he left my room. I exhaled deeply not aware I'd been holding my breath. I could feel how wet he'd made me. Between simply looking like his handsome self and feeling his gaze on my breasts, I had become pretty turned on.

I didn't do as he asked. How could I? He'd practically seen all of me now. My breathing was labored, and I was horny as hell. There was no way I was going to be able to act normally now.

Deciding I would stay in my room, I shut my door and turned the music back on. What's the worst that could happen? I locked the door this time to make sure it couldn't happen again.

Time passed. I can't be sure of how much. I felt Connor's hand on my hip and jumped sky high. Instead of laughing, he spun me around to face him.

"How did you-" I started to ask. My door was locked. I made sure of it. There was no way he could've got in my room.

He cut me off before I could finish my question by pressing

his lips on mine. He laid me on the bed, unfastened my jeans and slid them off before I realized his hands were below my waist.

I didn't stop him. Didn't make even the weakest attempt.

Connor spread my legs apart and buried his face between them. No one had ever gone down on me before, so I was unprepared for the almost unbearable pleasure his tongue flicking my clit provided. I gripped my comforter with my hand and moved to position myself better.

He grabbed my hips and pulled me closer to his mouth. My ass was off the bed, and I struggled for support. Using his shoulders, he maneuvered my legs over them. Once I caught on to what he was doing, I planted both feet on either side of his head and bucked into his face.

A small groan escaped his lips, and the sound sent me over the edge. I began to cum hard. I could feel my body convulse, and the walls of my labyrinth gripped to find something to hold onto that wasn't there.

As soon as my orgasm slowed, he stuck a finger inside of me then two. He never took his mouth off my pussy. With his other hand, he rubbed my clit. My second orgasm came seconds after the first. It would've gone on like that I'm sure if he hadn't moved away.

I thought he'd be undressing. I thought he would want reciprocation or was ready to fuck me. I was wrong. He walked across my room into the bathroom instead. That's how he got into my room.

"Hey," I said after him.

He paused in the doorway. "I'm sorry," he said.

'For what? I sure as hell ain't sorry about any of it.'

"We can't. Not while you're with Max."

'*Fuck. I forgot about Max,*' I thought. I collapsed on my bed and drifted off with dreams of Connor exploring every inch of my body the way I wanted him too.

Chapter Eight

I woke up with the taste of his kiss still on my lips. When I breathed in deep, I could inhale his scent. If it wasn't for the memory of him etched into my body, I would've thought last night was a dream.

There was a double ache between my legs. Part of it was a residual ache from the orgasm that rocked through me brought on by Connor's mouth. Mainly it was an ache of longing to feel him inside me. He'd given me a taste. Or rather, he had a taste of me. I wanted more. I wanted all of him.

When I woke the next morning, I thought for a minute I might have been dreaming. I actually had to check my diary to make sure it had really happened. Even then, I briefly considered maybe I wrote up a fantasy in my diary, but no, it was real. Connor and I made out last night.

Made out is an understatement. We almost had sex. Is oral considered sex? I wasn't really sure. If I was single, we would've had sex. Ugh. Max! He didn't deserve this. I trust Connor won't tell him. But now what?

This is not a situation I've ever been in before. It's been rare for one guy to have an interest in me, much less two at once. Two hot guys? Forget it.

I hurried up and got ready to catch Connor before he left for school. It was Friday. I had a date with Max planned, and Connor had a meet. If I didn't talk to him before he left, it'd have to wait until tomorrow. I needed to know what was going on between us. I needed to know if I was breaking up with Max.

When I walked into the kitchen, Connor was already there. It wasn't like him to be downstairs so early. As soon as he saw me, he gulped down his glass of juice and grabbed his book bag. I got the feeling he had been trying to avoid me and was going to hurry out the door now that I was there.

"Hey," I said.

He forced a smile and nodded at me while slinging his bag over his shoulder. "See you later," he said, turning to leave.

"Wait," I said louder than I had planned.

Connor stopped and turned to face me. He didn't say a word, and I regretted opening my mouth.

"I was hoping we could talk before school."

"I really have to get going," he lied.

He was trying to avoid me. "No, you don't," I said sternly. "You just don't want to be around me." I heard my voice crack, and I cursed my body for failing me.

"No, it's not that," he said.

I didn't look at him. I couldn't without crying.

Connor set his bag back down and took my hands. He leaned down to look up at my face from below. "Look at me," he said gently.

I closed my eyes and took a deep breath before lifting my head.

"I thought maybe it would be best for us to take a day or two to let things settle after what almost happened last night. That's all. If that's wrong, I'm sorry."

"So you don't want to be with me?"

Connor dropped my hands and leaned against the counter.

"Tiff," he said, staring at the cabinets. "You're with Max."

"That's exactly why I wanted to talk to you this morning. To see what I'm doing."

"What do you mean?"

"Well, if you want to be with me, I'll break up with him tonight."

Connor pushed off the counter and looked at me. He was clearly angry. "You think that's what I want?"

My heart sank. I knew it. Someone like Connor would never want a loser like me.

"You think I want to be the reason Max gets dumped? No, I don't want you to break up with him to be with me. If you don't want to be with him, that's one thing. But if you don't want to be with him, why haven't you dumped him yet?"

He grabbed his bag and started to walk out of the kitchen. "I think you need to decide what you want," he said, stopping briefly. "I don't want to be anyone's rebound, and I don't want to be the guy that broke up another couple."

My head was spinning. I didn't understand. Last night, he told me. He said, 'If you weren't with Max...' Didn't he? I couldn't be sure anymore. I thought he wanted to be with me, and maybe he does. Still, he's basically telling me it's not a possibility. Even if I break up with Max, it won't happen.

I went to school vowing not to waste another minute on Connor Newton. I was a straight A student. I had a full scholarship to my choice of colleges. I had a good looking boyfriend. Fuck Connor. Who needs him? Sure as hell not me.

That night I didn't even notice that Max seemed a bit distant. I was too preoccupied in my thoughts about how I wasn't going to dwell on Connor anymore to sense there was a problem. After our movie, he drove around for a bit, and I convinced him to find a spot to park. He didn't go to the usual spot we used when his mom was off work. I was too clueless to pick up on the signs. I should've seen what was coming, but instead I found it exciting. Instead of fucking in the back of his car on some secluded country road, I was getting hot thinking about making out in a grocery store parking lot where anyone could catch us.

Max let the car idle, and I leaned over to kiss him. He broke it off fairly quick and told me he wanted to hang out a minute and talk. I put one finger to his lips and let my other hand wander to his groin.

He tried to stop me, but I ordered him to let me. I was confused. I was angry at Connor. I needed to know where Max really stood in my life. And most importantly, I was horny as hell. This was going to happen.

My assertiveness worked, and Max relaxed, letting me take control. In fact, I think he was quite excited by how much I took charge. I took his cock out of his pants and sucked on it for a minute. When he was fully hard, I climbed across the front of the car and straddled him in his seat. I balanced myself in the air long enough for him to rip the package open and slide the condom down his shaft.

Once he was ready, I lowered myself down and let his cock slide in to my eager pussy. I closed my eyes and rode his shaft like my life depended on it. I thrust down on him hard and danced my hips around on him.

All the time I had Connor in my mind. I was fucking him in my room. After he finished eating my pussy, I didn't let him disappear through the bathroom. I grabbed him and threw him across my bed and climbed on top taking control. It was Connor bringing me to multiple orgasms even if it was Max between my legs.

I felt him buck and twitch and knew he was through. I slowly slid off him and back to the passenger side of the car. From lessons learned the hard way, I had a handful of tissues in my purse that I used to clean up. When I was done and had straightened out my clothes, I peered out the windshield wondering how no one had noticed us. Not a single person was ogling in our direction.

It took a few minutes for us to get collected. The silence was eerie. Max was never this quiet. "So, what did you want to talk about?" I asked, hoping to kill time while I built up the nerve to dump him.

"I'm not sure it's a good idea now," he said quietly.

"What?"

Max shook his head. "The timing's off after that. It can wait."

It took all of two seconds for it to hit me. "Timing? After sex? What *did* you want to talk to me about Max?" I asked. I admit it probably sounded like I was angry, but I assure you that I wasn't.

"No-nothing," he stammered. "It's fine."

"You were going to break up with me, weren't you?" I asked point blank.

He opened his mouth to object, but didn't say a word. He slunk back in his seat and crossed his arms over his face.

Got to give him credit for trying to be decent and not dumping me right after he fucked me. It was more than I was going to do. "Why?" I asked. "I thought we had fun together."

"We do!" he answered quickly. "I love hanging out with you. You're like a great... Friend," he confessed. "I'm really into you, but you always seem so distant. I feel like you'd always rather be somewhere else. Even when we have sex, I feel like you're not really in the moment with me."

"I'm sorry," I said quietly. He was not wrong.

"Sorry?" he asked.

"You're right. I enjoy being with you, but I don't think I feel the way I'm supposed to feel."

Max smiled at me. "You're not mad I did this after what we just did?"

"Nah, I kind of insisted anyway."

He took me home, and I couldn't wait till I could tell Connor. I was free to be with him. I tried to play it cool around Max, but once in my house, I burst with joy. Everything had clicked into place for once. The smile on my face was short lived.

Chapter Nine

Now what?

I had replayed our conversations in my head all day long the day after I was dumped, trying to figure out what I missed. There was nothing. Either I completely didn't hear something that was said, or I was, in fact, right about this.

Connor told me we couldn't be together while I had a boyfriend because he didn't want to be what broke up a relationship. He also said he didn't want to be a rebound. If he had mentioned the rebound thing today, I could almost see it. Max and I had only dated several weeks. It wasn't some deep, meaningful, all consuming love affair. There shouldn't be a rebound period. It certainly wouldn't be a lengthy one.

That's not what he was concerned about though. He didn't want to be the cause of the break up. Max broke up with me! It had nothing to do with Connor.

Did I plan on breaking up with Max? Yes. Was I relieved when he did it for me? Yes. Does Connor know what my intention was? Absolutely not.

When I got home last night, I waited up for Connor. I couldn't wait to tell him. I showered to erase all traces of Max from my body. It was my third shower of the day. I had one before our date to get ready as well. In my mind, I saw Connor embracing me as soon as he learned I was free to be with him. He'd carry me through my bedroom to my bed and ravish my body all night long.

The only possible explanation I can come to is that he never actually wanted to be with me. I don't know if the kiss, both times, were lapses in judgment, product of opportunity, or worse. Maybe it was desperation. No, it couldn't be that. Connor could get any girl he wanted. The kisses were a mistake. Period. He regretted making out with me and used Max as his excuse. He was still trying to use Max as his excuse now that we were over even though it no longer made sense to do so.

Either way, it didn't matter. Not really. Max dumped me, so that saved me from making a huge mistake. I would be single right now with or without Connor playing mind games on me. I was no worse off than I would've been anyway.

Days passed into weeks, and I slowly turned back into my usual sullen, sulky self. I spent my evenings studying way more than I needed to while sitting alone in my room. I narrowed down my college choices to two and was coming close to the deadline to make a decision. I fantasized a lot about getting the fuck away from this suck ass place. I thought about re-creating myself as someone new when I went off to school. I also fantasized at night in my bed, but not about Connor. He had lost his appeal to me. I thought about actors and singers and made up future college boyfriends to bring me to orgasm.

I still saw Connor on occasion. Sometimes he'd be around the house when I came through for one reason or another, but I never even glanced his way. There was the rare night when he was actually home when we ate dinner. I was polite to him for my mom's sake, but not friendly. Otherwise, I stayed in my room even on the nights when he was home hanging out downstairs, especially on the nights he was home.

Eventually, Connor confronted me for avoiding him. It didn't have to be this way, and he asked if I was always going to treat him like this. I gave some smart ass answer about how it wasn't because come August, I'd be gone. I'd be away to college in a different state never to have to deal with his ass again.

He told me he thought I wanted to be with him. The fucking nerve! He knew I did. "You rejected me, remember?"

"I want you more than anything," Connor said. "I know Max broke up with you because he didn't think you were into him."

"That's on him. I did nothing to make him feel that way."

"Even so, how would it look? If we got together right away, everyone would think something had been going on between us the whole time you were with him." He was mad that I didn't see it myself. "Plus I didn't want to be a rebound. I told you that. You could've just chilled out for awhile instead of showing your ass like this."

"How long is the rebound period? Huh? Max and I dated four weeks, not quite that long actually. It doesn't take months to get over someone, especially someone I was never really into. You've never made a move. Not once."

"How fucking could I? You were too busy letting me know you were still pissed at me every chance you got?" he was yelling.

"What about now?"

"Now what?"

"If you really want me like you say you do," I said, closing the gap between us. "Why not fuck me now?" I placed my hands on his chest and started to run them down toward his waistline.

Connor grabbed my wrists and gently pushed me back. He stormed off to his room and slammed the door.

What an asshole. I knew he was full of shit. I didn't know

what I was to him, but I was never going to be his girlfriend. I've been available all this time without him showing any interest at all. Even just then as I handed my ass to him on a silver platter, he rejected me again.

Chapter Ten

The way he ran out on me told me there wouldn't be a repeat performance ever again. I wasn't sure if I'd ever figure out what had been going on in that thick head of his over the last couple months, but I was certain he didn't know for sure himself what he wanted to do. If I spent the time overthinking it like I normally would, I'd have come to the conclusion that he wanted me. He just didn't want the scrutiny at school of not only fucking his step-sister for real, but fucking me specifically. Luckily, I didn't waste my time thinking about it.

Connor wasn't the only guy to show interest in me. A couple others at school had started appearing more and more in my messages and showing up at my locker to say hi between classes. Once again, I had my step-brother to thank for the newfound interest from them. And once again, I came to the conclusion that if Connor didn't want me, there was someone else who did.

That is exactly where my mind was at when I left the house that afternoon to meet Kara. The weather had finally broke, and the first party of the spring was happening at the creek near the old mill. This was the first time I'd been invited, and I was dragging her along for support. We spent hours doing outfit changes and perfecting our makeup before heading out. We took separate cars to ensure we could have all the fun we wanted without having to worry about if the other had a ride home.

It didn't take long for someone to swoop her up when we

arrived. Neither of us knew the guy very well. He went to school in a neighboring town. When he asked her to walk down the bank with him, I was genuinely happy for her even if it meant I was left all alone.

Minutes passed before I was approached by someone I had never seen before. His name was Greg, and he'd graduated two years earlier. This was no high school boy. Greg was experienced. The throbbing between my legs began keeping its own tempo almost immediately. I already had a few drinks. Maybe a drink too many. I almost asked him to find a place a little quieter to talk because the wait for him to do it was taking too long, but he finally whisked me off away from the crowd.

Once we found a secluded spot, Greg's hands began traveling my body before my feet came to a stop. I was wrong about the experience assumption, but what he lacked in skill, he made up for in confidence and eagerness. We sank to the grass several feet into the trees from the bank, and I was about laid back on the ground when I felt Greg's body leave mine.

When I looked up, I was thrown into shock and embarrassment. Connor was there pulling Greg by the collar and screaming at him to leave his sister alone.

'You've got to be fucking kidding me!'

As Greg made his retreat, Connor yanked me off the ground and half dragged me toward the field scattered with vehicles. He lectured me the entire way about giving myself too freely, being used, and not having any self-respect. When we were close to his dad's pickup truck, the realization of everything that was happening started to sink in, and I pulled away.

"Where do you think you're going?" he demanded, pulling me back toward him.

"Back to the party," I said. "You're not my fucking boss. You're barely my step-brother. I don't have to listen to you."

"You're... You're..." He couldn't finish the thought. His face was flush red with anger, and I could only imagine the thoughts swimming in his head.

"I'm what?" I asked, breaking free from his hold.

"You're mine," he declared.

"What?" I asked certain I heard him wrong.

Connor lifted me up and carried me to his dad's pickup. He opened the driver's door with one hand and practically threw me across the bench seat. He didn't move me over to slide in though. Instead he began to unfasten his jeans, and he pulled my ass down the seat closer to him.

"You're mine" he repeated, reaching under my skirt and grabbing my panties. He yanked them down and off my legs with such force they left inches long burns on both my legs that I didn't even begin to feel until much later. I didn't mind. Nor did I mind that my panties stretched out and ripped slightly in the process.

Once his pathway to my entrance was free, he wrapped one arm underneath me and held me still while he guided his cock between my legs with his other hand. He gave me one long lingering look. I couldn't be sure, but I think his eyes were saying, "Speak now or forever hold your peace."

I gripped his shoulders with my hands and tried to pull him down on top of me. He thrust forward, and I felt my step-brother's knob drill into me. He pulled back and thrust again so forcefully he barreled his full length inside my labyrinth.

My head fell back and a small gutteral scream escaped my throat. It was painful and pure bliss all in one fluid motion. He continued bucking into me hard. With each thrust, he pulled me back toward him with the arm that was beneath me to make sure the full length of his shaft drilled into me at full force. I was already cumming.

This was it. This was the fantasy. Connor Newton was fucking me like he owned me in the twilight of a field in his daddy's pickup truck. The shouts and laughter from the other students at the party could be heard as their voices carried across the breeze to us. At any moment, one of them could walk through the trees and catch us. It only served to heighten my pleasure knowing we could be seen.

"I've wanted this for so long," he said, staring into my eyes.

My mouth fell open to speak, but the only thing I could manage was more moans as he brought me closer and closer to another orgasm.

"You forced me to wait," he said, pulling out and flipping me over before I realized what he was doing.

I climbed up on my knees, expecting him to take me from behind, but he pulled my legs out from under me. It knocked me flat on my stomach, and I decided to lay there, knowing he'd place me where he wanted me.

"Max was one thing," he said, pulling me closer to the edge of the bench seat. "Knowing you were out fucking him. Knowing you were choosing him over me."

"That's not-" I started to say. He leaned over my back and brought his face down to mine, kissing me to stop me from speaking.

When he pulled back, he threw my skirt up over my back and rubbed my ass cheeks with both hands. "Then you just couldn't wait, could you?"

He moved again, and I wasn't sure what he was doing because I couldn't see him. Then I felt his mouth. His lips moved delicately across my ass, and he spread my cheeks apart. When his tongue touched the taut button of my ass, my instinct was to move away, but the sensation that shot through me kept me in place.

I moaned. Connor was in total control. I was his. I was at his mercy.

"I was doing it for you. Waiting for the timing to be better. Keeping you from more rumors, but you couldn't see that. You're happier running around, giving it up to everyone except the one man who loves you."

'Loves me? What?' I wanted to ask. I wanted to be sure. I couldn't. If I had heard him wrong, I didn't want it to be corrected. Then the sharp, fiery pain hit.

I hadn't even noticed Connor moved his mouth away from my ass. I was so preoccupied with his confession of the heart. The tip of his cock was slowly invading my virgin ass.

"Connor!" I cried without a thought.

"Oh, Tiff," he moaned. "I've been dreaming about this. Dreaming about the day you give all of yourself to me."

I squeezed my eyes shut tight and bit down on my hand. I couldn't say no to him. Not to my step-brother. Not to the one man I wanted but shouldn't. Not to the one man to ever proclaim his love to me.

His cock eased past the opening of my ass, and the pain lessened. Slightly. He continued forward as far as he could then pulled back and drove his cock into my ass again. The movements stayed slow and steady, and once his rhythm was strong, he burrowed his hand under me to tease my clit.

The added stimulation sent the fireworks off in my labyrinth. The walls of my pussy began to clench.

"Oh, Tiff," Conner groaned. "I knew you'd love this. I can feel your pussy convulse against the walls of your ass."

Minutes later, his breathing changed, and he began to shake. I knew he was shooting his load inside me. He collapsed forward onto me for several minutes.

When he moved again, he stood up and straightened his clothes. I rolled over to fix my outfit, carefully sitting on the side of my leg as my ass screamed if I put pressure on it.

I looked up and Connor was staring at me. He was waiting for me to say something, to say anything to reassure him. I took his hands and pulled him close. I touched my forehead to his and kissed him gently.

"What do we do now?" he asked.

"Let's go home."

"Home?" he looked puzzled.

I smiled at him, and said, "Yeah. Let's go where we can do this again in private."

He grinned, and I heard him exhale deeply in relief. He kissed me again while pushing me across the bench to climb inside. Then he drove us home in record time.

More by Darling Coxx Available everywhere and on Kindle Vella!
The Nanny Diaries Series
Nanny Diaries #1

Lacey Moore bit off more than she could swallow when she took the position at the Wyndham estate. What was supposed to be the perfect job accompanied by great hours, pay and perks like living rent free in the guest house soon turned out to be more than she had could have ever imagined. The main duties of her job included making sure the entire staff stayed satisfied, and it was a job she intended on doing well.

Nanny Diaries #2

Vicki Sweet didn't know what she was walking into when she took the job as nanny for the Rayburn's. Soon she found herself loaded with maid duties as well as chasing after the children while Lance worked and ignored all of his wife's illicit activities. Tori Rayburn needed to be put in her place, and Vicki was just the woman for the job. Chasing after Tori's affairs, Vicki began stealing them away one by one, but her eye remained on the ultimate prize. Vicki would have her saucy way with Lance before her job ended, and once she set her mind on something, she always got what she wanted.

Nanny Diaries #3

Mindy Cummings didn't except anything from Mark Jacobs expect a decent paying part time nanny job that worked well with her college schedule. The apartment over the garage for her own private affairs was an added bonus. She soon learned how little she knew about the man she'd been babysitting for since she was a teen. It wouldn't take long to realize that his touch was the one thing she needed more than anything. Fantasy after fantasy, he filled her thoughts. His face was who she envisioned no matter who she was with. The one thing she didn't expect was for fantasy to become reality.

Family Secrets Series
Lex's Education
Tiff's Fantasy
Natalie's Secret
Abby's Night
Sylvia's Fresh Start
Supernatural Erotica
True Love's Kiss
Nightstalker

Deadly Sins
Pride
Greed
Spring Break Affairs
Obeying Orders Series

About the Author

DARLING COXX IS A SEASONED writer who has been featured in many major publications under her given name. Taking a break from interviews and personal experience pieces, she is trying her hand at short novellas in the same genre she's been working in for most of her life.

Her adult entertainment career began while working as the manager of an adult store. It is her favorite position of any she's held, before or since. It was there where she made the contacts that allowed her to venture into the world of adult entertainment both in her own writing as well as producing a few pieces of her own.

Please feel free to reach out to her at DarlingCoxx@gmail.com. Follow her on Instagram and Twitter @DarlingCoxx to stay updated on future publications.

www.ingramcontent.com/pod-product-compliance
Lightning Source LLC
Chambersburg PA
CBHW030845200726
48285CB00007B/2559

9 781952 422256